This LITTLE MAMMOTH belongs to

_____

_____

_____

More DILLY titles, for older readers,
are available from Mammoth

Dilly the Dinosaur
Dilly's Muddy Day
Dilly Tells the Truth
Dilly and the Horror Film
Dilly and the Worst Day Ever
Dilly and the Tiger
Dilly and the Ghost
Dilly Dinosaur, Superstar
Dilly the Angel

Tony Bradman lives in Kent with his wife and three
children. He has written many children's books and also
reviews for *Parents* magazine.

Susan Hellard lives in North London. She has illustrated
several books for Mammoth including the previous
Dilly titles and the lift-the-flap book *Time To Get Up*.

DILLY
SPEAKS UP

DILLY
SPEAKS UP

by
Tony Bradman

illustrated by
Susan Hellard

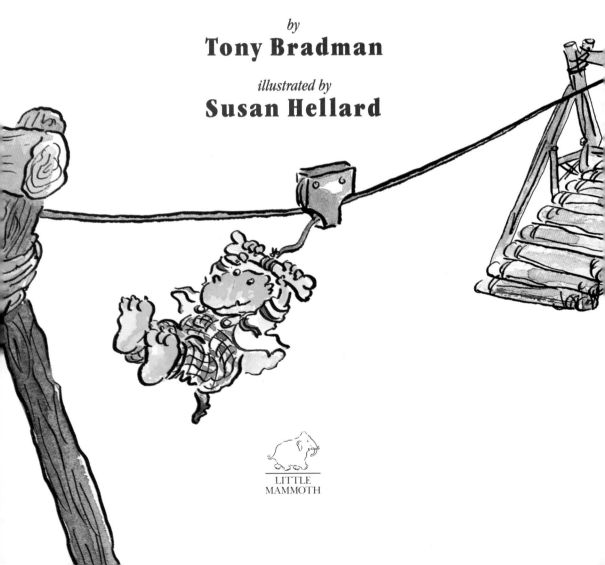

LITTLE
MAMMOTH

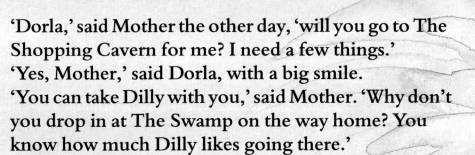

'Dorla,' said Mother the other day, 'will you go to The Shopping Cavern for me? I need a few things.'
'Yes, Mother,' said Dorla, with a big smile.
'You can take Dilly with you,' said Mother. 'Why don't you drop in at The Swamp on the way home? You know how much Dilly likes going there.'

'I'll only take you to The Swamp if you promise to do what I say,' said Dorla. 'Now come and get ready like a good little dinosaur.'

'I promise,' said Dilly. 'But I don't want to wear *that* coat...'

'Dilly...' said Dorla.

Dilly put on the coat.

'Dilly,' said Mother, 'I want you to be on your best behaviour. And remember, Dorla's in charge. She has a list of things to do.'
Dilly opened his mouth, but Dorla spoke first.
'He'll remember, Mother,' she said.
'Good,' said Mother. 'Make sure you're careful...and Dorla, be home by 12 o'clock.'

As they walked down the street they met Mr
Darma, their neighbour.
'Hello, Dilly,' he said. 'Going somewhere nice?'
Dilly opened his mouth, but Dorla spoke first.
'We're going to The Shopping Cavern,' she said.
'And if he's good, I *might* take him to The
Swamp afterwards.'

When they arrived at The Shopping Cavern, Dilly saw his best friend Dixie.
'Hi, Dilly,' said Dixie. 'Look what I've got...'

Dilly opened his mouth, but Dorla spoke first.
'I'm sorry, Dixie,' she said, dragging Dilly away, 'but
Dilly hasn't got time to talk just now...'

'One large jar of swamp worms, please,' Dorla said to the dinosaur in the food store.
'Do you like candied fern flakes?' he asked Dilly. 'I loved them when I was your age.'
Dilly opened his mouth, but Dorla spoke first.
'He can't,' she said, 'he's not to eat anything between meals.'

They had to go to the post office next. Inside, Dorla
met some of her friends.
'So you're Dorla's little brother,' one of them said.
'Aren't you sweet!'

Dilly opened his mouth, but Dorla spoke first.
'He's not so sweet once you get to know him,' she said.

At last it was time to go to The Swamp. A police
dinosaur helped them to cross the road.
'You look excited,' she said to Dilly, who was bouncing
up and down.
'And where are you off to?'
Dilly opened his mouth, but Dorla spoke first.
'He won't be going anywhere unless he behaves
himself,' she said.

But when they arrived at The Swamp, Dilly got a nasty surprise. 'We haven't got time to go in it,' said Dorla, pointing at the clock.

'Mother said we had to be home by 12.'

'But I *want* to go in The Swamp,' said Dilly.

'Well Mother says I'm in charge, and you'll do what I say,' said Dorla.

'No, I won't. I don't have to listen to you,' said Dilly. He opened his mouth...

...and let rip with a 150-mile-per-hour, ultra-special, super-scream, the kind that makes everyone dive into the bushes until he's finished. And when he stopped screaming, he started to cry.

'OK, Dilly,' said Dorla, who felt a little guilty. 'You can have five minutes in The Swamp. I suppose you have been good. But that's all.'
Dilly had a wonderful time.
'I'm going to tell Mother you were horrible to me,' he said on the way home.
Dorla didn't say anything.

'That wasn't so bad, was it, Dorla?' said Mother
when they got home.
'Wouldn't you like to take Dilly out again some
time?'
Dorla opened her mouth, but Dilly spoke first.
'Of course she would, Mother!' said Dilly with a
smile.
He looked at Dorla...and they both laughed.

First published in Great Britain 1990
by Piccadilly Press Ltd
Published 1991 by Little Mammoth
an imprint of Mandarin Paperbacks
Michelin House, 81 Fulham Road, London SW3 6RB

Mandarin is an imprint of the Octopus Publishing Group

Reprinted 1991

Text copyright © Tony Bradman 1990
Illustrations copyright © Susan Hellard 1990

The right of Tony Bradman to be identified as Author
and Susan Hellard as Illustrator
of this work has been asserted by them in accordance
with the Copyright, Designs and Patents Act 1988

ISBN 0 7497 0666 X

A CIP catalogue record for this title
is available from the British Library

Printed in Great Britain
by Scotprint Ltd, Musselburgh